Young Cam Jansen

and the
Molly Shoe Mystery

A Viking Easy-to-Read

BY **DAVID A. ADLER**

ILLUSTRATED BY **SUSANNA NATTI**

VIKING

For Natalie Grace Zellner—happy reading
—D.A.

To Uncle Bill
—S.N.

VIKING
Published by Penguin Group
Penguin Young Readers Group, 345 Hudson Street, New York, New York 10014, U.S.A.
Penguin Group (Canada), 90 Eglinton Avenue East, Suite 700, Toronto, Ontario, Canada M4P 2Y3
(a division of Pearson Penguin Canada Inc.)
Penguin Books Ltd, 80 Strand, London WC2R 0RL, England
Penguin Ireland, 25 St Stephen's Green, Dublin 2, Ireland (a division of Penguin Books Ltd)
Penguin Group (Australia), 250 Camberwell Road, Camberwell, Victoria 3124, Australia
(a division of Pearson Australia Group Pty Ltd)
Penguin Books India Pvt Ltd, 11 Community Centre, Panchsheel Park, New Delhi – 110 017, India
Penguin Group (NZ), 67 Apollo Drive, Rosedale, North Shore 0632, New Zealand
(a division of Pearson New Zealand Ltd.)
Penguin Books (South Africa) (Pty) Ltd, 24 Sturdee Avenue, Rosebank, Johannesburg 2196, South Africa

Penguin Books Ltd, Registered Offices: 80 Strand, London WC2R 0RL, England

First published in 2008 by Viking, a division of Penguin Young Readers Group

1   3   5   7   9   10   8   6· 4   2

LIBRARY OF CONGRESS CATALOGING-IN-PUBLICATION DATA
Adler, David A.
Young Cam Jansen and the Molly shoe mystery / by David A. Adler ; illustrated by Susanna Natti.
p. cm. — (Young Cam Jansen ; 14) (Viking easy-to-read)
Summary: When Cam, her father, and friend Eric go to the airport to meet Cam's Aunt Molly,
they help her find her missing shoes.
ISBN 978-0-670-06142-6 (hardcover)
[1. Lost and found possessions—Fiction. 2. Aunts—Fiction. 3. Airports—Fiction. 4. Shoes—Fiction.
5. Mystery and detective stories.] I. Natti, Susanna, ill. II. Title.
PZ7.A2615Yrm 2008
[E]—dc22
2007031181

Viking® and Easy-to-Read® are registered trademarks of Penguin Group (USA) Inc.

Manufactured in China
Set in Bookman

CONTENTS

1. Aunt Molly Quacks

"I like your aunt Molly,"

Eric Shelton told his friend Cam Jansen.

"She's so funny.

Once, I said hello to her

and she said, 'Quack!'"

"Molly works for an airline,"

Cam's father said.

"She flies so much

that sometimes she feels like a duck.

That's why she quacks."

It was a sunny spring day.

Cam, Eric, and Cam's father

were on their way to the airport.

Aunt Molly was coming to visit,

and they were picking her up.

Cam's father parked his car.

"We're late," he said.

He hurried through the parking lot.

Cam and Eric followed him.

Mr. Jansen stopped by the door

to the arrivals building.

"Oh, my," he said.

He turned and looked

at all the cars in the parking lot.

"I already forgot where I parked our car."

"Don't worry," Cam said. "I remember."

Cam closed her eyes and said, *"Click!"*

Then, with her eyes closed, she said,

"Our car is in section E4.

It's parked between a red car

and a blue van."

Cam has an amazing memory.

"It's like a camera," Cam says.

"I have pictures in my head

of whatever I've seen."

Cam says *Click!* is the sound

her camera makes.

Cam's real name is Jennifer.

But because of her amazing memory,

and because she says, *"Click!"*

people started calling her "The Camera."

Soon "The Camera" became just "Cam."

"Good," Mr. Jansen said.

"We'll find our car.

Now let's find Aunt Molly."

2. "I Know You"

Cam opened her eyes.

She and Eric followed Cam's father

into the building.

Just inside, the sun was shining

through many large windows.

"I'm sorry," Eric said.

"The sun is in my eyes.

I can't see, so I can't find Aunt Molly."

"Shade them," Mr. Jansen said.

Mr. Jansen held his hand above his eyes.

Cam and Eric shaded their eyes, too.

They looked across the large room.

Along one side were small shops

selling newspapers, candies,

flowers, and balloons.

In the middle were chairs.

The chairs on one side of the room,

the side in the sun, were empty.

The shaded side of the room was crowded.

"There she is," Eric said.

He hurried across the room.

He stopped by a woman who was reading.

Eric said, "Hello, Aunt Molly."

The woman looked up.

"Oh," Eric said. "You're not Aunt Molly."

The woman laughed. "Yes, I know."

Eric looked for Cam.

She was with her father.

They were talking to someone.

"Oh, there she is!" Eric said.

"Bye," he told the woman who was not Aunt Molly.

"Bye," the woman said.

Eric hurried to Cam.

"I'm a tired duck," Aunt Molly said.

She rubbed her eyes.

"I wanted to stretch across a few chairs," she said.

"But this side of the room is too crowded."

Mr. Jansen asked, "What about the other side?"

"That's too sunny," Aunt Molly told him.

"I tried, but I couldn't rest."

"Let's go," Mr. Jansen said.

"You can rest at home."

"Hey," Aunt Molly said to Eric.

"I know you. You're Cam's friend.
You're Elroy."

"I'm not Elroy," Eric said.

"Leroy?"

Eric shook his head.

"My name is Eric Shelton."

"Oh, hello, Sheldon. I'm Molly Jansen."

Cam laughed and said,

"Hello, Leroy Sheldon."

Eric and Mr. Jansen laughed, too.

Aunt Molly got up

and started toward the door.

"Let's go," she said.

"What about your suitcase?"

Mr. Jansen asked.

"Let's take it," Aunt Molly said.

"And what about your shoes?" Cam asked.

Aunt Molly looked down. "Oh, my," she said.

"I'm not wearing them."

3. China, Chile, and Peru

"Hey," Aunt Molly said.

"I'm wearing pretty socks."

She wriggled her toes.

"But where are my shoes?

They're my favorites.

They're red with shiny gold buckles.

They were made for me in London."

Aunt Molly turned to Eric and said,

"You know, Sheldon,

that's a long way from here.

It's a big city in another country."

Aunt Molly smiled and told Eric,

"Call me if you want to go to London.

I sell airline tickets."

"Molly," Mr. Jansen asked,

"where are your shoes?"

Aunt Molly looked down again.

She wriggled her toes and said,

"I don't know."

Eric said, "Some people take their shoes off when they rest."

"That's what I do," Aunt Molly told him.

"I'll look for them," Cam said.

Cam went back to where
Aunt Molly had been resting.

She looked under the chair.

Then she hurried back.

"I found these coins," Cam said.

"But I didn't find your shoes."

"Oh," Aunt Molly said.

"The coins dropped from my pocket.

I brought them for you.

They're from different countries—

from China, Chile, and Peru.

Please share them with Sheldon."

Cam kept a few coins.

She gave a few to Eric.

"Thank you," Eric said.

Then he asked Aunt Molly,

"Did you rest on the airplane?"

"Yes. I always do."

"Then that's where your shoes are,"

Eric said. "You left them on the airplane."

4. Pebbles and Puddles

"Maybe I did leave them there," Aunt Molly said.

Mr. Jansen said, "Let's go back and

look for them."

Aunt Molly's suitcase had wheels.

She pulled it through the terminal.

Cam, Eric, and Mr. Jansen followed her.

They all went to the airline's information desk.

"Hello, I'm Molly Jansen," Aunt Molly said.

"I was on flight number . . .

I was on flight number . . .

What flight was I on?"

Hi everyone!
I can't wait to see you all next week.
Is it next week? Yes, it is. Here's the flight information: I'll be on flight 72 and it's supposed to arrive at 6:15 p.m.
See you soon!
love,
Aunt Molly

"I know," Cam said. "You sent us an e-mail."

Cam closed her eyes.

She said, *"Click!"* and looked at the picture

she had in her head of Aunt Molly's e-mail.

"You were on flight 72."

"Yes," Molly told the man behind the desk.

"I think I left my favorite shoes on flight 72.

They're red with shiny gold buckles."

"I'll check," the man said.

He made a telephone call.

He waited and then shook his head.

Her shoes were not found on the airplane.

Aunt Molly slowly pulled her suitcase
toward the door.

"I loved those shoes," she said.

Aunt Molly was upset.

She didn't look where she was walking.

She stepped into a puddle of spilled soda.

"Now my socks are wet!"

Aunt Molly sat down.

"Please," she said to Cam, "bring me my suitcase.

I have to change my socks."

"Hey," Cam said. "There's a lump in your suitcase.

Maybe that lump is your shoes.

Maybe when you rested,

you put your shoes in your suitcase."

Cam brought Aunt Molly her suitcase.

Aunt Molly opened it.

"Look," she said. "It's cheddar cheese!"

Aunt Molly took out

a large wrapped block of cheese.

She took out a box of crackers.

"I love cheese and crackers," she said.

"Who wants some?"

"What about your socks?" Mr. Jansen asked.

"What about your shoes?" Eric asked.

Aunt Molly found a pair of socks

in her suitcase. She put them on.

She didn't find her shoes.

"I'll go without shoes," Aunt Molly said.

"I'll just look out for puddles and pebbles."

Aunt Molly started toward the door.

Cam, Eric, and Mr. Jansen followed her.

When Aunt Molly got near the door,

she shaded her eyes.

Cam stopped. Cam looked at the sun

shining through the windows.

She looked at Aunt Molly.

"Wait!" Cam said.

"I think I know where to find your shoes.

I think I solved the mystery."

5. "Let's Go Home"

"That's great!" Aunt Molly said.

"Now let's go home."

"Wait," Eric told her.

"First let's see if Cam can find your shoes."

Cam went back to the sunny side of the room.

Eric went with her.

Cam said, "When Aunt Molly shaded her eyes,

I remembered that she tried to rest here.

Maybe she took off her shoes.

It was too sunny, so she moved.

Maybe she left her shoes here

when she went to the shady side of the room."

Cam and Eric looked under the chairs.

They found newspapers and paper cups.

Then Eric reached under a chair

and pulled out a pair of shoes.

They were red with shiny gold buckles.

Eric brought the shoes to Aunt Molly.

"Are these yours?" he asked.

"Yes," Aunt Molly said.

Aunt Molly put the shoes on.

"Thank you," Aunt Molly said.

"Now let's go home."

Aunt Molly walked toward the door.

"Molly!" Mr. Jansen said.

"You forgot your suitcase."

Mr. Jansen pulled the suitcase

toward the door.

Then he stopped. "Oh, my," he said.

"With all this talk of shoes,

I forgot where I parked the car."

Eric said, "I'm sure Cam remembers."

Cam closed her eyes and said, *"Click!"*

"The car is in E4," Cam said.

"It's between a red car and a blue van."

Cam opened her eyes.

"Let's go," Mr. Jansen said.

"Let's go before someone

forgets something else."

"Yes," Aunt Molly said.

"This tired duck needs to rest."

A Cam Jansen
Memory Game

Take another look at the picture on page 31.

Study it.

Blink your eyes and say, *"Click!"*

Then turn back to this page

and answer these questions:

1. Are there more than eight people

   in the picture?

2. What color are Cam's pants?

   What color are Eric's?

3. Is Cam wearing a jacket?

4. Is anyone pushing a luggage cart?

5. Is Cam smiling? Is Eric?